Ghost of a Hanged Man

Ghost of a Hanged Man

Vivian Vande Velde

MARSHALL CAVENDISH • NEW YORK

Copyright © 1998 by Vivian Vande Velde
Marshall Cavendish Corporation,
99 White Plains Road, Tarrytown, New York 10591

Library of Congress Cataloging-in-Publication Data
Vande Velde, Vivian.
Ghost of a hanged man / written by Vivian Vande Velde. — 1st ed.
p.   cm.
Summary: An outlaw condemned to be hanged threatens to wreak vengeance
from the grave on those responsible for his death.
ISBN 0-7614-5015-7
[1. Ghosts—Fiction. 2. Brothers and sisters—Fiction. 3. West (U.S.)—Fiction.
4. Robbers and outlaws—Fiction.] I. Title.
PZ7.V2773Gh   1998   [Fic]—dc21   97-23773   CIP   AC

The text of this book is set in 12.5 point New Baskerville

Book design by Constance Ftera

Printed in the United States of America

1   3   5   6   4   2

To the Beatsons—not old friends,
but friends for a long time.

Contents

Ghost of a Hanged Man

Jake Barnette

Summer 1877

Pa said we were too young to go to the hanging.

That was fine with me. I didn't want to watch a man die, even if that man was Jake Barnette, famous outlaw who'd killed sixteen people. He was also accused of three train robberies and about two dozen bank holdups—not to mention cattle rustling and horse thieving. But Judge Wade said it was a waste of time to have any more trials, seeing as how Jake admitted he was guilty, and the state could only hang him once anyway.

My sister Annabelle, who's three years younger than me, was the one who was disappointed. "Aw, come on, Pa," she wheedled. "Elijah Quinn's whole family is going, and all three of his sisters are younger than me."

Annabelle had been two, and sound asleep, the

night Mama died. Jake Barnette's hanging was something else entirely, but I figured if I lived to be one hundred, I never wanted to see anybody die, ever again.

Pa looked at Annabelle over the tops of his glasses. We were the only ones in the office or he wouldn't have been wearing them because he said people wouldn't trust a sheriff who needed glasses, even if he only needed them for reading. "I said no, and that's my final word."

Pa has never been one to yell, but even Annabelle could catch on that maybe she'd asked once too often, and he was beginning to get mightily annoyed with her.

Still, she tried coming at it from a slightly different direction. "Well, can't you let Ben go?" she asked. "He's almost twelve, and that's old enough." No doubt she was hoping that if I went, I'd share all the gory details with her.

Pa looked from her to me, back to her again. I was shaking my head, but I don't think that made any difference. He said, "The first time I saw a hanging was when I was thirty, during the war, and *that* wasn't old enough. Now run along home, both of you. I've got these papers to finish."

Judging by his grim expression and the way he looked so tired, I guessed they were probably papers having to do with tomorrow's hanging.

"Come on, Annie," I said, tugging on her arm before she got us saddled with extra chores for a privilege I didn't even want.

Anyway, I figured our age didn't have anything to do with it. Pa didn't want us going because of what had happened at the trial.

Miss Hawkes, the schoolteacher, had decided it would be a good idea for all of us to go to the trial. "See our government in action," was the way she put it, though I reckoned she was mostly curious, just like everybody else, on account of Jake Barnette being so famous. Anyway, the trial went pretty fast, seeing as how everybody knew he was guilty, and the only surprise came at the end.

After the jury proclaimed Jake guilty, and after Judge Wade said he was to be hanged by the neck until dead, Jake stood up and asked if he could say something to the courtroom.

Judge Wade frowned. He said, "You've been given more than enough chances to speak out, and you chose to sit there smirking instead." But Judge Wade was a fair man, and so he relented. "All right, have your say. But make it quick."

"Oh, it'll be quick," Jake promised. Still, he turned around to look at the members of the jury and the spectators. Then he turned back to the judge. "You may kill me," he said. "But if you do, I'll come back. I'll take you with me."

In the moment of stunned silence that followed, he seemed to have all the time in the world to turn around yet again. "And you," he said pointing to Pa, who'd been the one to arrest him, "and you," he pointed to Mr. Chetwin, who'd been the foreman of the jury and who'd been the one to announce the jury's decision, "and—"

Judge Wade was banging his gavel like crazy, the crowd was all talking at once, and Emmett Sanders, Pa's deputy, grabbed hold of Jake's arm.

"And you," Jake told him, not shouting, not threatening, just soft and serious. "And all your families, too."

That, I figured, was the real reason Pa didn't want us going to the hanging.

2

The Hanged Man

Some of the townspeople were worried that Jake Barnette had friends who would try to rescue him the day of the hanging. Pa reminded them that Jake's two best friends were among the sixteen people he'd killed. They had been members of his gang, and Jake had shot them rather than divide the money with them. "Nobody's likely to come," Pa said.

Still, he spent the night at the jail, and he assigned Emmett Sanders to come to the house and stay with us.

No gang members showed up at our house, but Emmett *did* catch Annabelle trying to sneak out her window the morning of the hanging. Our bedrooms are on the second floor, but there's a big old elm she'd been known to use before.

I don't know if Annabelle figured Emmett would be easy to fool on account of his being young and new to the job, or if she hoped his age would make him more understanding. But Emmett marched us both to my room, which is on the opposite side of the house, with the closest tree being the one way over in Widow Haybecker's yard. He set a chair against my door, sat himself down, and read the newspaper right there in the hall.

"Drat!" Annabelle said.

"Well," I tried to encourage her, "no matter what they said, I'd bet some of the other eight- and nine-year-olds won't be going either. But you'll be the only one who can say it took an armed guard to keep you away."

It would be a good excuse for me, too, and nobody had to know that the armed guard and I thought alike on this.

The good thing about Annabelle is that—for as often as she throws a sulk—at least she can't keep it up long. "Elijah Quinn says he saw a bunch of hangings back in Kansas City before his family moved here," she said. "He told me sometimes, when the trapdoor falls away, the noose breaks the hanged man's neck, and then he dies right away. But sometimes it doesn't, and he strangles to death with his tongue hanging out, and that takes a lot longer."

"The trouble with you," I said, "is that you have no imagination."

"Do, too," Annabelle said. "I can picture that happening."

"So can I. The difference is, for me picturing it is bad enough. . . . I don't want to really see it."

"Baby," she taunted me.

"Gruesome toad," I retaliated.

Eventually Pa came home, which meant it was all over, and no sign of any of Jake's friends.

"Did his neck snap," Annabelle asked Pa, "or did he choke to death?"

Pa just shook his head in exasperation.

But Annabelle and I were sitting on the front porch when the Quinn family drove by in their wagon, last of all to leave because Mr. Quinn is the undertaker. Elijah caught Annabelle watching and held his clenched fist by his neck, then jerked his hand up, tipping his head way over to the side— which we guessed signified broken neck.

And, sure enough, that was all we heard about for the next few days. By the following week, it was old news, and by the week after that the whole business about the trial and the threats and the hanging didn't seem nearly as interesting as the fact that somebody's stray cat had had kittens under the front porch of the schoolhouse. Just about everybody forgot about Jake Barnette.

Until spring.

3

_____ **Tinkers**

Spring 1878

According to the calendar, it was spring, but the first time I saw any of the tinkers up close, the day was as cold and gray as winter.

There was still another hour of school, but Miss Hawkes had sent me on an errand to Pickett's General Store. Charity Pickett—perhaps the most badly misnamed girl in the whole town, with the possible exception of her older sister, Patience—had gotten sick. Charity said it was from Billy Empy tugging on her braids all morning and giving her a headache, and that Billy should be expelled because of it. I was inclined to believe it was more probably due to the fact that, as usual, Charity gulped her lunch down real fast before anybody could ask her to trade or share, and then she'd spent just about the entire recess time spinning around pretending to be a top and crashing into people. Whatever the cause, that afternoon Charity threw up all over her desk, herself, and Billy Empy's shoes. Then, after Miss Hawkes finished cleaning up the mess and asked Charity if she was feeling better now, Charity merely held her stomach and swayed greenly in her seat.

So that was how Miss Hawkes came to tell me to go find Mrs. Pickett or Patience, who was sixteen and no longer attended school, and tell one or the other of them to kindly come fetch Charity before she was sick again.

And that was how I happened to walk in Pickett's General Store and find myself in the middle of an uproar.

Mrs. Pickett was hollering, my Pa was there, a crowd was gathering, and the center of the problem seemed to be a pair of strangers I'd never seen before, a young man five or six years older than me, and a woman who—by the way she was defending him—had to be the young man's mother. She and Mrs. Pickett were going at each other looking ready to come to blows, Mrs. Pickett calling the woman a thief and the mother of thieves, the woman calling Mrs. Pickett a pig-faced witch.

"You're the witch," Mrs. Pickett said. "Dirty gypsy witch."

I sidled up to Patience and asked, "What's going on?"

"Tinkers," Patience told me with a sneer for my stupidity. "Gypsies."

I had guessed that already, by the stranger woman's flounced and brightly colored skirts. I knew a group of tinkers were camped north of the town on the river—seven or eight wagons that had been there all winter, which was longer than tinkers usually stay. But I hadn't been close up to any of them before.

My father was trying to calm the situation down. I could tell even though I couldn't hear what he was saying over the two women yelling at each other.

I was about to ask Patience for more details when Pa finally raised his voice to be heard above all the racket. "Quiet!" he demanded. "I said 'One at a time.' Mrs. Pickett?"

The tinker woman snorted and tossed her hair, which was all loose like a girl's. Her expression clearly stated she had suspected all along she wouldn't really get a chance to tell her side of it.

Patience leaned in to say to me, "Tinkers are good for raising good horses, and for fixing things and sharpening scissors and knives and such. But everybody knows they're thieves. That's why they never stay long in any one place: honest folk won't have them."

I hadn't noticed there were any other tinkers in

the room until someone beside me snorted, just like the tinker woman had done. It was a girl who looked younger than me but older than Annabelle, and she was dressed in similar fashion to the woman Mrs. Pickett was even now scolding for having raised thieves.

I felt bad about what Patience had said, since my asking was what had caused her to say it.

"Don't pay attention to Patience," I told the girl. "She hates everybody."

"Starting with you, Benjamin Springer." Patience snarled and stalked away from me.

The tinker girl didn't look impressed that I had defended her.

"Your mother and brother?" I asked.

The girl looked at me as though my brains were dribbling out my nose. "Uncle and great-aunt," she said, and turned her back on me to see what was going on with her kinfolk.

Just as I had lost Patience, so Pa was losing patience also. He told Mrs. Pickett, "Why don't you just tell me what happened."

"That gypsy boy"—Mrs. Pickett pointed at the young man—"come in here, touching everything, looking at everything, trying to decide what-all to steal."

"Mrs. Pickett," Pa said in his warning voice, "was anything stolen?"

Mrs. Pickett ignored that question. "And he knocked over that glass and broke it."

The other woman said, "He didn't break your glass. Why would he want to touch it? It's so ugly. He was standing right by me over here when it fell." She had an accent that gave her voice a nice singsong quality, despite the fact that she was shouting.

"He fooled with it before," Mrs. Pickett said. "So that it fell over later."

The tinker woman said something in her own language and made a gesture that I didn't recognize, but I reckoned most probably it wasn't polite.

I doubt Mrs. Pickett knew what it meant either, but *she* must have figured *Double you back,* for she repeated the motion twice, bigger and angrier.

Pa stepped between them with his arms outstretched to keep them from going at each other. "That's enough," he warned. He turned to Mr. Pickett and asked, "Jeremiah, what did you see?"

"I . . . ," Mr. Pickett drew the word out, not liking to contradict Mrs. Pickett—*nobody* liked to contradict Mrs. Pickett, "didn't see anything," he admitted.

Mrs. Pickett let her breath out in a puff of disgust.

"This woman here"—Mr. Pickett indicated the tinker woman—"was telling my fortune—"

"Heathen foolishness," Mrs. Pickett interrupted, "and a waste of good money."

Behind Pa's back, the tinker woman repeated her earlier gesture, and Mrs. Pickett again returned it two times.

"Be that as it may," Mr. Pickett said, "that was what she was doing. And when I heard the crash, I looked up quick, and the boy was standing by us, nowhere near the shelf."

Mrs. Pickett put her back to all of us, her foot tapping in frustration.

"Seems to me," Pa said, "occasional breakage is one of the risks storeowners take. You can't be accusing people of breaking things and stealing things just because there's nobody else to blame."

"Thank you, *Pastor* Springer," Mrs. Pickett muttered.

Pa just said, "Show's over: customers stay, everybody else out."

The tinker woman didn't look pleased, even though it seemed to me Pa had taken her side. She and her son left in a huff.

"You, too," Mrs. Pickett said to the little girl by me, "even though you've probably got half my inventory stuffed under that shawl of yours."

The girl held her arms out to indicate she wasn't holding anything.

Mrs. Pickett just said, pointing, "Out."

And the girl, looking in a snit, left, pausing only to curl her lip at me. As the people who'd come to see what the ruckus was began to clear out, I heard someone ask Mr. Pickett, "So, what did she say was in your future?"

The idea of anyone being able to see what the future holds never struck me as likely, so I was heading for Mrs. Pickett, to tell her about Charity. But I heard Mr. Pickett say, "Oh, it didn't make an awful lot of sense. Something about the town being in danger from the water."

"Town usually doesn't have *enough* water," someone commented, as Mr. Pickett continued, "And drowning people, or drowned people, coming up out of the water, and people in boxes . . ."

"Oh, people in boxes," someone laughed. "Newest thing from Philadelphia, I hear. Did you and Mrs. Pickett order some?"

I laughed, even knowing I had Mrs. Pickett to face yet, because it struck me as funny. At the time.

A Very Rainy Spring

The further along spring got, the worse it rained. It rained more than anybody in town could remember, and some of those people were the ones who'd built the place to begin with. The river overflowed, houses in the low-lying areas flooded, the farmers insisted they were ruined, and there was mud everywhere. Miss Hawkes—only half-smiling—read us the story about Noah and the Flood.

But then school got canceled because Miss Hawkes's family was one of three whose houses collapsed because of the shifting mud, and she had to go help her parents rescue what they could of their possessions.

Annabelle and I were alone at home when Elijah Quinn came knocking at our door. "You have to see this," he said as soon as I opened the door. Rain was pouring down his face despite the sad, floppy hat he wore.

"Didn't your parents ever teach you to come in out of the rain?" I asked, and I stepped back to let him in.

But: "You have to see this," he repeated, never making a move to enter. He looked, in fact, as though he could barely contain himself from grabbing hold of my arm and dragging me out there with him. "Annabelle," he called spotting her behind me, "get your coat on."

"Why?" she and I asked together.

But Elijah wasn't about to tell. "Un-huh," he insisted, "it's something you have to see for yourselves."

"Too wet," I said, thinking about the unavoidable puddles that would come in over the tops of our boots, and the rain that would drip down our collars, and how—if either of us got sick—Pa would hold me responsible. Though I was curious.

"It's worth it," Elijah insisted.

"Worth it for two nine-year-olds," I asked, "or worth it for a twelve-year-old?" Behind me, Annabelle was already getting her coat.

"Worth it for *any*body," Elijah said.

Hard to fight that much enthusiasm. "It better be," I grumbled, and went for my own coat.

Annabelle, of course, had it worst, with her long skirts dragging through the mud, then slapping the backs of her legs; but I wasn't much happier.

Only Elijah was grinning as we hunched ourselves against the wind and rain.

"Where are we going?" I asked as we headed down the street. We went past Pa's office, where—the day was so gray and dismal—an oil lamp shone in the window even though it was only lunchtime.

"You'll see," Elijah said.

We went past the school, past the church.

"You'll see" was all Elijah kept repeating, until I was ready to strangle him.

We ended up at the cemetery.

The rain and the river spilling its banks had half the cemetery under a new-formed pond, which was kind of interesting, but didn't account for all the townsfolk scurrying about: adults as well as children.

Elijah didn't explain, waiting for us to catch on by ourselves.

We moved closer, the mud sucking at our boots. There was mud all over, and not just mud, but churned up mud, like . . .

I stopped. For a second I had thought someone must be getting buried in this awful weather, even though I hadn't heard of anybody dying. But the ground was just too churned up, there where the new pond met the ground. Like a whole batch of graves had been dug. Or like . . .

"The coffins are coming up," Elijah explained,

once he saw that we could see. "The ground is so soaked, they're just working their way up to the surface."

I looked around quick, but Mama's grave was up on high ground, nowhere near to being in danger.

We moved closer still.

There were planks of wood lying around all over the place, spread out, and people were walking on them. Sidewalks—of a sort—I realized, to keep people from sinking in the mud.

Mr. Quinn was there, with Samuel, Elijah's older brother, and Mr. Montgomery from the hotel. They were carrying a coffin, moving it out of reach of the still-spreading water. That's what a lot of the people were doing, although not everybody was as organized as Mr. Quinn, who was, after all, the undertaker, and used to carting around dead bodies. I heard him chewing out the Kingsfield bothers, saying to be sure to mark the coffins clearly before moving them, or they'd never keep straight whose was whose.

"Look." Elijah led the way, picking a path along the zigzag of boards. The wood was slick with mud. He pulled me to a place where one corner of a coffin was just working its way through. "Here's Mr. Haybecker. Think he's lonely for his wife?"

"*Here's* one you can practically see the person," Annabelle said, heading for a coffin that was caved in. But that was more wishful thinking than truth: we couldn't make out anything. We didn't recognize the name, and the date was nearly forty years past.

Some of the people milling about weren't so much helping as just keeping an eye on things, like Mr. Chetwin, whose wife was still buried, but her neighbor on the left-hand side was more than halfway out. I don't know if that was another of Mr. Chetwin's relatives, but he sure was cranky about the whole situation. He yelled at us to stop hanging around and go home.

"Hanging!" Annabelle cried. She whirled to face Elijah. "*Hanging*. Where's Jake Barnette buried? Is he still underground?"

A slow grin spread over Elijah's face, and he pointed right in the direction where there was the most destruction.

There was the plain pine coffin I'd seen on the back of the Quinns' wagon, completely unearthed, stained dark with rain and mud. The marker was flat on the ground beside it.

Annabelle got off the boards, circling the coffin, trying to find a knothole to get a good peek. Neither her shoes nor her dress was ever going to be the same again. Then, "Um, Ben?" she said. "I think I'm stuck."

I looked down and saw that the mud completely

covered her feet, making her legs look like they ended at her ankles.

"*Now* what are you going to do?" I asked. It was her own fault for being such a little monster.

"Come on, Ben." She wiggled her fingers at me. "Help."

I reached, but she was too far, even when I stood as close to the edge of the board as I dared.

"Afraid of getting your shoes dirty?" Elijah asked in a superior voice. He stepped off the board and immediately sank in as deep as Annabelle. "Oh," he said. "Now I see the problem."

Tempting as it was to leave them both there, I hauled Elijah back onto the board.

To Annabelle, I said, "Think you'll be all right while I run home to fetch some rope? Maybe fix myself a cup of something warm to drink to take off the chill?"

"Very funny." She wiggled her fingers again, knowing I wouldn't really abandon her in Elijah Quinn's care.

I saw a stick jutting out of the muck, and I yanked that out. "Here, grab hold of the end of this."

Annabelle did, and I tugged. I tugged it right out of her hand. "You're supposed to hold on," I told her.

"You pulled too hard," she complained.

"If I don't pull hard, how will I pull you out of the mud?"

"Pull hard," Elijah advised, "but not too hard."

"Now why didn't I think of that?" I muttered. Though Annabelle didn't complain, I saw her rub her hand on her dress and guessed that the stick, which had all little bumps and twigs coming out of it, must have hurt. I saw a better one, shorter, but smooth. "Hold on tight," I told her. I pulled, and pulled . . .

"I'm losing my shoe," she cried.

She was about to let go, I could tell. "We'll get it later," I assured her, and the next moment she was falling against me, safe up on the board.

"Yay!" Elijah said.

"My shoe," Annabelle said. At least she'd only lost one.

The place where her foot had been was already filling in, but I jabbed the stick in where the mud was still indented and fished the shoe out.

"Yay!" Elijah said again.

I wanted to smack him on the side of the head with the muddy, ruined thing, but I restrained myself.

"Thank you," Annabelle told me, lifting the shoe from the end of the stick.

I saw Elijah's eyes suddenly go wide. "That's not a stick," he cried. "That's a bone!"

I let it drop fast.

Elijah bent in for a closer look. "Oh," he said. "My mistake. I guess it *is* a stick."

I wished I'd hit him while I had the chance.

"Hey, you!" someone shouted, so close we knew it was for us. Mr. Chetwin came running up, shooing us away. It was quite a sight because Mr. Chetwin was about as big around as any other two townsfolk. He waddled as fast as his short legs would carry him, and his face was all red like he was about to explode. "Get away from there. Go on, you young hoodlums, go home." He looked slightly past us, then added, "Can't you control your children?"

I hadn't even recognized Pa, all bundled up but soaked and covered with mud. He and Emmett Sanders were apparently helping out because he said to us, "You're too little to make yourselves useful, so you'll have to keep out of the way." He touched the side of his hat, by way of apology to Mr. Chetwin. Then he put Jake Barnette's wooden grave marker on top of the coffin, and he and Emmett picked the whole thing up and moved off toward higher ground, tottering and balancing on the planks of wood.

"Sorry, Mr. Chetwin," each of us said, one after the other: "Sorry, Mr. Chetwin," "Sorry, Mr. Chetwin," "Sorry, Mr. Chetwin"—not really meaning it, not really sure what we were supposed to be apologizing for.

He walked off in a huff without answering.

"What do you think he's more worried about?" Elijah asked. "His wife coming back or Jake Barnette coming back?"

I didn't think he was worried about either. I thought he just hated children.

But that was the first in a long time I remembered Jake at the trial, threatening to take us with him: Mr. Chetwin, Judge Wade, Emmett Sanders, Pa, Annabelle, and me.

5

Zandra

I figured Annabelle was cold and wet enough—even though she wouldn't admit it—that I better get her home. Elijah was still hoping for someone to drop one of the coffins and have it split open, so he decided to stay a bit longer.

I had my hat pulled down to protect my eyes from the stinging rain, and I was holding on to Annabelle because we were facing into the wind and she was having trouble making headway, when we walked smack into someone.

I had a brief impression of someone about Annabelle's height, and of bright-colored skirts and bare feet. And then the person was falling off the wooden planks of the sidewalk and into the mud of the street. She yelled something in some foreign language I didn't understand, then switched to English. "Idiot! Clumsy fool!"

It was the tinker girl I'd seen last month in Pickett's General Store.

"Sorry," I said, even though she'd been half running, with the wind pushing at her back; she had walked into me just as surely as I had walked into her. I reached down to give the girl a hand up, but she slapped my arm away.

Still, when she tried to stand, her feet slid out from under her and she landed, once again, bottom first in the mud. The second time I offered my hand, she took it.

"Why don't you have a coat?" Annabelle asked her, because the girl wore only a shawl.

I smacked Annabelle's arm, figuring the girl's family was probably too poor to buy her a coat. I saw no call to be making her feel bad on account of her people being poor.

But tactful Annabelle continued: "And it's too cold for bare feet."

I smacked Annabelle a second time.

"What?" she demanded.

The girl tossed her long black hair over her shoulder, revealing bright earrings. "I was doing fine until you knocked me into that river that passes for a street in this town of yours," she said. She wasn't doing fine now; her teeth were chattering.

"Is your family nearby?" I asked.

"Yes, of course. They're sitting right here on

the sidewalk. Can't you see them?"

I felt my cheeks go red with embarrassment. "I meant: do you have anybody here who can bring you back"—*home* didn't seem right—"someplace dry?"

The girl sniffed, more cold than upset, I judged. "My papa and my uncle are seeing about selling some horses. We're getting ready to break camp before the river floods where we are, and I was just sightseeing one last time in this lovely little swamp of yours when you flung me into the mud."

She was older than Annabelle, I decided, judging by her biting sarcasm. Probably closer to my age, despite her small size. I considered just apologizing again—or not—and leaving her there, but I felt responsible. Not as responsible as she wanted me to feel, but responsible.

"Our pa's office is just two doors down," I said. "You're welcome to come in and dry yourself off by the stove." That would be good for both her *and* Annabelle.

She hesitated, probably trying to think of a witty response, but the wind swirled around for a second just then, blowing at least a bucketful of rain off the roof and onto us, and she nodded.

Inside Pa's office, her dark eyes got big at the sight of the jail cells—empty at the moment—and she said, "Your papa must be the sheriff." The sign over the door said that, so she must not have been able to read. I pinched Annabelle's arm before she could say anything, and I just said, "Yes." Then I said, "My name's Ben Springer. And this is my sister, Annabelle."

"I'm Zandra," the girl said.

"What kind of name is that?" Annabelle demanded as she and I took off our coats.

"It's a princess's name," our guest said. Her bare feet tracked wet, dirty footprints from the door to the stove, where she turned her back and raised her skirt to dry the backside of her underskirts, which was just about the most un-princesslike thing I'd ever seen, but I didn't say so. She shook her skirts to unstick them from her legs, and something fell from a pocket, a small package, wrapped in a scrap of red cloth.

I leaned down at the same time Zandra did, and our heads cracked together. "Yow!" I said, rubbing my head.

Zandra snarled at me in her foreign language again, and Annabelle reached in to pick up the package.

The cloth came loose and pieces of paperboard fell from Annabelle's hand.

"Playing cards!" Annabelle cried in delight. I could just guess she was about to suggest playing old maid, which was her favorite game, because she always won—because she always cheated. But Zandra was saying, "You aren't supposed to touch those," at the same time Annabelle took a closer look and said, disappointed, "Not playing cards."

I got a brief glimpse of strange, bright-colored, pictures before Zandra grabbed the remaining cards from Annabelle's hand, then swooped down and scooped up the ones off the floor.

"How can you play cards if you can't touch them?" Annabelle demanded as Zandra rewrapped them in the piece of red silk.

"They're not cards to play with," Zandra said. "And *I* can touch them. *You* can't."

"What's the use of touching them, if you can't play with them?" Annabelle asked, obviously pleased with her own logic.

"They're for telling fortunes," Zandra said.

I was too polite to scoff, though maybe I should have, because Annabelle believed her. "You can tell fortunes?" she asked, wonder in her voice. Then, before Zandra could finish saying, "Yes," Annabelle said, "Can you tell my fortune?"

"Are you willing to pay?" Zandra asked.

"Yes," Annabelle said, at the same time I said, "No."

Annabelle dug into her pocket and came up empty-handed. Naturally she turned to me. "Oh, please, Ben," she begged. "It'll be fun. Please, please."

Zandra was watching me with an expression that said she knew I was too cheap. It was her certainty that made me say, "How much?"

"A penny."

I figured a penny was worth it to keep Annabelle from jumping up and down.

So I handed Zandra a penny. She moved to Pa's desk and sat down in his chair, wet skirts and all. Annabelle and I moved in behind her to look over her shoulder.

6

In the Cards

Zandra pushed Pa's papers aside to form a clear spot. She laid one card down and said, "This is you," and began to shuffle the remaining cards. I could see the set-aside card was labeled PAGE OF CUPS, though I would have called it a jack.

"Me?" Annabelle asked with a frown.

"Ben," Zandra said, looking back over her shoulder at me.

"*I'm* the one who wanted my fortune told," Annabelle protested.

"*He's* the one who paid me."

I could figure that one out: Annabelle was still going to demand to know her fortune after mine was told, and Zandra would charge a second penny.

Before I could say a word, Zandra said, "It's too late now." She smiled sweetly, setting cards out. She dealt ten of them around the one she'd said was me, then looked at them, frowning.

I figured she was concentrating, trying to make something up. Annabelle asked, "What's wrong?"

Zandra shook her head and showed me the cards she hadn't dealt. "Most of the cards have these symbols on them: swords, cups, pentacles, and wands."

Swords were, of course, swords, cups were old-fashioned drinking goblets, pentacles were stars, and wands were wooden poles. They were sort of like regular playing cards because they were numbered. But where normal cards would have things like the five of hearts or the seven of spades, in Zandra's cards, the symbols were part of a picture. As Zandra fanned them out for me to see, I spotted the two of pentacles, which had someone juggling two stars, and the three of cups had three women dancing around, each holding a cup.

Zandra continued, "But half the cards I dealt for you are these kind: a picture without one of the four symbols. That means a powerful outside influence—someone or some *thing* controlling what will happen to you. And the other half are all swords, which means conflict."

"What's this one mean?" Annabelle asked, tapping one of the cards with her finger.

"Don't touch," Zandra told her. "That's the

Devil." She glanced at me. "He stands for violence. Black magic."

"Ben being a bad boy," Annabelle finished.

"No," Zandra said. She stared at the cards, her eyes darting back and forth as though she were searching for something. Or as though she didn't like what she was seeing.

I didn't like what I was seeing. I pointed to a card that had someone lying on the ground with ten swords sticking out of his back. "Is this supposed to mean I'm about to die?" I tried to make it clear how stupid I thought all of this was, but I'm not sure it came out sounding that way. Nobody likes to think of dying.

"No," Zandra said. "Bad luck. Maybe tears and pain. Not necessarily death."

Not necessarily. How reassuring.

"What about—" Annabelle started.

"Would you be quiet and let me read the cards?" Zandra snapped.

Annabelle and I looked at each other.

Zandra bit her lip. "These are not good cards," she admitted. "See, this one with the ten swords is the one which covers you, it's the major influence. This one which crosses that is the Star, which *is* good. That means hope, and love which will help you."

"Oooo, love," Annabelle cooed.

"But then here's the Three of Swords, reversed—"

"What does 'reversed' mean?" I asked.

"Upside down. The Three of Swords, reversed, says that someone from your past might cause you sorrow. And this one—" Zandra tapped her finger on one of the picture cards, "Judgment. But that's reversed, too, which means . . . weakness."

The way she hesitated, I was willing to bet it meant more. I turned the card to see it better. Zandra opened her mouth to complain, but before she got a chance, I gasped in surprise. "What?" she asked.

"The picture."

"It's the Day of Judgment," she said. "People rising from their coffins."

"And the coffins rising from the water." I couldn't help but shiver. "That's what's happening. Here. In town. Today."

Still she was looking at me blankly.

"The river overflowed, and the coffins are coming up out of the ground."

Her eyes opened wide in shock. "It's not my fault," she said.

I tried, unsuccessfully, to make sense of that. To break the silence I finally told her, "I never said it was."

As though I'd argued with her, Zandra insisted, "Just because somebody predicts something, that's entirely different from causing it to happen."

"Well, sure," I agreed. "And, besides, you just set this card out. The coffins have been coming up since last night."

"Yes." Zandra drew the word out. But then she bit her lip and looked all worried again.

I can be real slow, but usually I *do* eventually catch on. Eventually. "Oh," I said. "You're thinking of your great-aunt, who predicted . . ." I was going to say "Jeremiah Pickett's fortune," but then I remembered how it had been more than that. Bad times for the town, he had reported her saying. Drowned people coming out of the water. And drowned people were certainly dead, if they were drowned all the way. And she'd said something about people in boxes, and we'd all pictured paper boxes, like gifts come in. What we'd seen this morning all fit, sort of, what she'd said a month ago.

Zandra watched me work all this out.

I said, "People can't affect the weather. Not by wishing, and not by predicting. Why, if people could do that, they'd always predict good weather for themselves, so there'd never be failed crops."·

"No," Zandra agreed in a little voice.

Annabelle, who hadn't been in Pickett's store, wasn't following this. She was still looking at the cards Zandra had set out. She asked, "Who's this upside-down man?" and Zandra didn't hush her. Zandra said, "That's the Hanged Man."

Annabelle and I both nearly choked on that one. We hadn't had that much experience with hanged men, so Hanged Man meant only one thing to us.

"He just means a change," Zandra explained. "That could be good or bad."

Knowing Jake Barnette, I figured bad.

Annabelle told Zandra about Jake, and about his promise to come back and take certain people with him. Annabelle finished by saying, "It sounds to me, with all these bad things, as though Jake might be coming back for Ben."

"That's silly," Zandra said. But she didn't sound as though she thought it were silly.

"What about this blindfolded lady surrounded by swords?" Annabelle asked.

"The Eight of Swords," Zandra mumbled. "Doubt. Not knowing which way to turn."

"And the King?" I asked.

"Your fate is in someone else's hands."

"Jake Barnette's," Annabelle said knowingly.

"That's stupid," Zandra and I chorused.

I wished either one of us sounded more convinced.

7

Annabelle's Turn

"Well, that was certainly worth a penny," Annabelle said cheerfully, little ghoul that she could be. "May I have a penny for my reading now?" she asked me.

Hoping to improve the mood, I gave her a penny, which she handed to Zandra.

Zandra gathered up the cards and looked through them. "This is you," she said, much more quietly, much less sure of herself than before. The card was once again the Page of Cups.

"Why can't I be a Queen?" Annabelle asked as Zandra shuffled.

"You're too young. Children are pages, and I picked cups for both of you because cups stand for water, and that's all there is in this town." The instant she said it, she looked like she wished she could take it back, as though she were still afraid we'd blame the town's misfortune on her and her people.

She dealt out ten cards.

Annabelle got five picture cards, too, but only one sword.

"Hanged Man," I pointed out, in case Annabelle hadn't noticed.

She didn't say anything, but stuck her tongue out at me behind Zandra's back.

"This is a very good card," Zandra said, skipping over the first and going straight to the second. "This is the Hermit, which means you'll meet someone who will guide you."

Annabelle can't be sidetracked that easily. "What's this one mean?" she asked, backing up one.

"The High Priestess." Zandra shook her head. "Hard to say. She's silence and mystery, a hidden future, shaped by hidden influences. This one—"

"Is Death," Annabelle interrupted, sounding suddenly scared. The card showed a skeleton riding a horse.

"It means change," Zandra stated firmly.

"Just like the Hanged Man." Annabelle's mouth twitched nervously.

It was one thing for me to tease her, it was another to have her really scared. "Good change or bad change?" I asked.

But apparently that wasn't a good question, because Zandra looked away before answering, once again, "Hard to say." She took a deep breath. "This Five of Cups isn't bad," she continued. "It means loss. . . . Do you see these three spilled cups? But not all is lost, because there are two cups still standing."

Annabelle didn't look very encouraged. She skipped to the one cheerful-looking card of the bunch. "What does the last one mean? That one looks nice and calm." It was a man gazing out from a castle tower, looking fat and rich.

"But it's reversed," Zandra said softly. "It means being ruled by others."

Just then the door flew open, and all three of us jumped. But it was only Pa, wet and muddy. He grinned to see us.

"Pa, this is Zandra," Annabelle announced, her fear forgotten already. "She was telling our fortunes."

Zandra was hurriedly gathering up her cards.

"Was she?" Pa said. I knew he didn't believe in that sort of thing, but he was too polite to say so.

"Tell Pa's fortune," Annabelle said.

"No, I don't think so." Zandra's hands were shaking as she tried to align the cards, and she dropped them back on the desk and had to start over. She was probably just nervous about Pa being sheriff, I thought. He'd gone to the tinkers' camp a few times, when people had complained about things being stolen: mostly chickens, and clothes off laundry lines.

"Oh, please," Annabelle wheedled.

"Annie," Pa warned, "she said no."

"But it's only fun," Annabelle insisted. "Isn't it, Zandra?"

I was close enough to see Zandra's face, to see that it was more than just fun to Zandra. But she didn't want to say so, not after the fortunes we'd gotten.

"Please."

Zandra removed the King of Cups and placed it down on the desk, never even asking for another penny.

Good thing.

She got no further than dealing out the Hanged Man and a tower that had been struck by lightning and was bursting into flame, when she scooped the cards back up and said, "I have to go now."

She shoved the cards into her pocket, not even taking the time to wrap them in their silk covering, but just jamming the cloth in after them. Then, tightening her shawl around her, she ran outside, even though it was still raining.

Pa looked after her, then turned to us. "Was it something I said?" he asked.

"Hard to say," I answered.

In the Dark of the Night

I woke up in the middle of the night, sweating hard, breathing hard, my heart racing. The instant I woke up, I knew I'd had a real bad dream, but I couldn't remember what it was.

On the other hand, I had the strongest feeling that whatever the dream had been about, and whatever had awakened me, the one thing I definitely did *not* want to do was turn my head on the pillow and look out my window. The longer I thought about it, the more sure I was that somebody—or something—was watching me.

My skin felt all prickly, as though it wanted to crawl right off my body and hide someplace safe.

Whatever was out there, I told myself, no matter how terrible, surely it was better to turn and face it rather than let it come up behind me. Except, of course, that if I *didn't* turn around, I could pretend it wasn't there.

Right up until the moment it would grab me.

I forced myself to move my head, and even then it took several long seconds before my already-opened eyes could see, which had little to do with the dark, and much to do with being too scared to see straight.

Nothing. Just the night sky.

Taking a deep breath, I swung my legs over the side of the bed.

Still nothing.

I walked to the window and knelt on the clothes chest that served as a window seat.

Still nothing. How could there be? The bedrooms are on the second story, and on this side of the house there aren't any nearby trees to climb up.

The rain had finally stopped, and the clouds had melted away, so the moon and stars lit the empty yard and the smooth, white-painted side of the house.

Nothing.

There was no such thing as people being able to tell fortunes—despite Zandra's great-aunt's lucky guess—and there was no danger to me that Zandra had seen, and there was nothing outside.

Then I heard a floorboard creak. And footsteps. From inside the house. Approaching my door.

It took all my courage to cross the room. The

door was already closed, and I considered pushing my dresser in front to barricade it, but there wasn't enough time; the footsteps were just about even with my room.

Take the offensive, I thought, and I flung the door open.

Pa, walking by in his long underwear, jumped back with a gasp. "Boy, I'm an old man," he said, though he wasn't *that* old. "My heart can't take much more excitement tonight."

"What?" I asked.

"Annabelle had a bad dream," he explained. "She woke me up with a scream, but when I didn't hear a sound from you, I figured you'd slept right through it."

Maybe Annabelle screaming was what woke me up. Or not. No way to be sure. I'd been so concentrating on what was or was not outside my window, I hadn't heard Pa go to her room or comfort her, but had only become aware of him as he made his way back to his own room.

"Is she all right?" I asked. Horrid as she could sometimes be, I didn't want anything bad to happen to her.

"Can't even remember what scared her."

I nodded. "Sorry I startled you," I said.

He patted me on the shoulder. "Goodnight, Ben."

I closed the door.

Fortune-tellers, I thought. *Giving gullible people nightmares.*

It was plain foolishness.

But I was glad the night was bright, and it took me a long time to fall back asleep.

9

Mr. Chetwin

Not having gotten much sleep, I was still in bed when Deputy Emmett Sanders came banging at our door early next morning.

By the time I was dressed, he was gone. "What is it?" I asked Pa. Pa was sitting at the kitchen table, pulling on his boots.

"Ira Chetwin died during the night," he said.

"Murdered?" I asked, having Jake Barnette on my mind.

Pa snorted. "More like fifty years of eating too much, drinking too much, and taking everything too seriously."

I remembered how red in the face he'd been about me and Annabelle and Elijah being underfoot at the cemetery. Mr. Chetwin was always red in the face.

Pa said, "He'd hired the Kingsfield boys to paint

his house once the rain stopped. They came knocking on his door first thing in the morning. No answer, but they got to work anyway, which is a surprise no matter how you look at it, considering the Kingsfields. But, anyway, they started scraping the old paint from around the windows, and when they got to his bedroom window, they looked in and there he was, lying in bed with his eyes wide open. Doc Fitzgerald says his heart probably gave out during his sleep."

"Bad night all around," I said.

Pa looked at me real stern. "A man dying is nothing to make mock of, Ben." He was on his feet before I had a chance to say that wasn't my intent.

Still, I wasn't the only one to think of murder. Elijah Quinn came over to ask if Annabelle and I thought Jake Barnette had something to do with Mr. Chetwin's sudden death—which did more to convince me he hadn't than anything Pa or Doc Fitzgerald could have said.

But adults were talking about it, too.

I'd gone to Pickett's General Store—partly with a craving to buy a penny pickle from the barrel, but also to get away from Annabelle and Elijah. A lot of other people were out and about too, celebrating the good weather, and several of them were gathered in Pickett's before me.

"Anybody else notice," somebody pointed out

just as I came in, "that—with Ira Chetwin being a widower who never had any children, and with Emmett Sanders being both real young and an orphan—Sheriff Springer is the only one of the townsfolk Jake threatened who has any family?"

Suddenly that pickle craving just dried up and blew away.

"What about Judge Wade?" someone asked. "Is he married?"

Nobody knew. Nobody thought so, but nobody knew.

Judge Wade was a circuit judge, traveling from town to town to those places that weren't big enough to have their own regular court, so Pa was probably the only one who knew him real well; and Pa wasn't one to hang around the general store gossiping.

"The judge is due in tonight," one woman said. "I'll ask Betsy Montgomery if she can't find some way to ask him."

Just about then, somebody noticed me in the crowd, and the conversation quickly shifted to the weather, and what a relief it was that the rain had finally stopped—"*Despite*," Mr. Pickett said, "that gypsy woman's curse."

It wasn't a curse, I wanted to tell him. *You never thought it was a curse before.* But I figured if I said such a thing, I'd get swatted and told to mind my manners to my elders. And they *still* would believe what they wanted to believe. So I said nothing. But the only interesting thing I heard after everybody finished complaining about the tinkers was the estimate that it would probably be at least another two days before the ground dried out enough to start reburying the unearthed coffins.

That evening after supper, Annabelle suddenly asked Pa, "Is it all right if I sleep in your room tonight?"

Pa looked up at her with a scowl, which was more surprise than annoyance. "No," he said.

"Then, may I sleep in Ben's room?"

"No," Pa said again. "Why are you asking?"

"No reason," Annabelle said with a shrug.

Naturally, Pa figured I was to blame. "Have you been telling tales to scare your sister?"

"No, sir," I assured him.

"Out with it, girl," Pa commanded.

Annabelle shuffled her feet. "Elijah Quinn said"—and I could hear Pa sigh just at that little bit—"that nighttime is when ghosts are strongest, and that's how Jake Barnette was able to get at Mr. Chetwin and scare him to death. Elijah says that's what stopped Mr. Chetwin's heart."

Pa rested his face in his hand and shook his head. "There's no such thing as ghosts, Annie," he said. "And you're too old to be believing in them, or to be sleeping in other people's rooms."

"Yes, Pa," she mumbled.

Pa looked at her for a long couple of seconds, then reached over to the mantelpiece and took down the photograph of him and Mama and me, when I was four years old, and Annabelle, when she was too young to walk or talk or listen to Elijah Quinn. Annabelle's foot was blurred in the picture because she'd been too young to understand when the photographer said we had to hold still. "Would you feel better if you had this up in your room with you?" Pa asked. "If you knew Mama was watching over you?"

Annabelle brightened up. She nodded vigorously and took the picture. "Good night, Pa," she said, giving him a big hug and kiss.

I gave Pa a look behind Annabelle's back, which was supposed to say that I thought Annabelle was a baby.

But if there had been a second picture of Mama, I wouldn't have said no to having it in my room.

10

Another Dark Night, and a Darker Morning

I had trouble going to sleep that night, what with thinking about Mr. Chetwin dying, and trying to convince myself that a lot of people had died throughout the history of the world with no help at all from Jake Barnette, and worrying about Zandra's foolish fortune-telling cards, and wishing someone had tied and gagged Elijah Quinn before he'd gotten around to telling my sister—and she'd gotten around to telling me—that ghosts are strongest at night.

There were certain things I just couldn't get out of my head: the way Jake turned around at his trial, looked Pa dead in the eye, and said, "And you"; the way Zandra's Day of Judgment card with its coffins coming out of the water looked just like what I had seen not fifteen minutes earlier at our own cemetery; the way I'd been so sure last night that someone had been watching me from my window.

It's hard to say what was remembering and what was dreaming. I'm not sure if I dozed at all. But I know I was awake when I realized I wasn't just remembering what last night had felt like—I was feeling it again.

"Dunce," I whispered it out loud for scaring myself silly. But it was like sitting in school and realizing you have an itch, and you don't dare scratch because Miss Hawkes is right in the middle of yelling at everyone for all their fidgeting and foolishness, and the more you try not to think about it, the more it itches.

I told myself there was no reason to look out that window, but I just couldn't convince myself.

So I turned my head real slowly . . .

. . . And saw a dark shadow looming right on the other side of the glass.

I was too scared to even call out for help.

It's just a shadow from a tree, I thought.

Except, of course, there are no trees on that side of the house.

I forced myself to get out of bed, to approach the window. As I moved, the shadow broke up and disappeared, so that by the time I got there, there wasn't anything to see.

Just something about the angle of the window glass, I told myself. *And the way I turned my head, and the fact that I was half-asleep, and the fact that I'd gone to bed with scary thoughts.*

I got back into bed, but I didn't lie down. I pulled the blankets up around me and sat facing the window until somehow, despite my best intentions, I fell asleep.

The following morning I staggered groggily into the kitchen as Pa was making coffee. He took one look at me and didn't bother with "Good morning." At least Annabelle looked well rested and cheerful.

"No more nightmares?" I asked.

She shook her head. "Mama kept them away."

I figured Annabelle's confidence had more to do with it than Mama did.

"So," I said to Pa, subtly moving the conversation in the direction I wanted, "I understand Judge Wade was scheduled to come to town yesterday."

"Yes, and he arrived safe and sound." Pa looked up at me over the edge of his cup. "Interested in the law profession all of a sudden, Ben?" he asked.

I squirmed under his knowing gaze. "I heard some people talking yesterday, and they were trying to remember if Judge Wade has any family."

"People with time on their hands will talk about

anything." Pa shook his head. "Like that the tinker women caused the river to flood."

Seeing how put out he sounded, I didn't ask him if he thought there could be any truth to that: not that anybody had *caused* it to happen, but whether he guessed people—some people—could *tell* what was going to happen before it did.

Pa got back to the question I'd started with. "Judge Wade is a lifelong bachelor," he said. "And in case you're interested in his opinion as well as his marital status, he thinks this worry is a lot of superstitious nonsense."

"Are you sure?" Judge Wade came from Boston, and he'd gone to school at Harvard. I figured someone with that much education probably knew what he was talking about, and that made me feel better.

Pa nodded. "Samuel Quinn 'just happened' to drop by the office yesterday about three seconds after the judge arrived."

"And?" Annabelle prompted him.

"Ask Samuel's little brother, Elijah: the judge laughed him out of the office."

Which was even more encouraging.

Until Emmett Sanders came knocking at our door again.

Even Pa looked a bit troubled as he went to let

Emmett in for the second early morning call in two days.

"You better come to the hotel," I heard Emmett say to him. "It looks like some time during the night Judge Wade fell down the stairs and broke his neck."

11

Jake's Fortune

"Can we come?" Annabelle asked as Pa headed for the door.

"No. Finish your breakfast."

She and I exchanged a glance. Without a word, we each knew that we both chose to read that as: No, *not until* you finish your breakfast.

So we gulped our food down, then ran to Montgomery's Hotel. There was a crowd outside—*kept* outside by Deputy Sanders—but those who'd been there awhile were eager to share what news there was with any newcomers.

There are several boardinghouses in town, but only one hotel. And it isn't like a big-city hotel with someone at the desk all night long. So no one had seen Judge Wade fall. But he *was* dead. That was about all anybody knew—despite all the talking and all the guessing that was going on.

Then Doc Fitzgerald came out.

"Dead for hours," Doc Fitzgerald announced.

"Dead of what?" somebody called out.

"A broken neck," Doc answered.

"Just like Jake Barnette," said some who had been to the hanging.

Doc ignored that.

Next out was Mr. Montgomery, the owner of the hotel. He wanted to make sure everybody knew the hotel was perfectly safe, no loose boards or slippery steps or lodgers who'd sneak up behind you and give you a push or anything like that, which may or may not have been comforting news, depending on your outlook.

"Any *tinkers* come in?" someone shouted out.

"No," Mr. Montgomery said. He added that his room was right on the first floor in case there ever were any late-night callers; and he said—now that he thought about it—he'd probably heard the judge fall. He'd assumed it was some animal dumping the kitchen scraps that had been put out in the alley.

Pa came out about then and shooed the crowd away. "It was an accident," he said. "Unfortunate, but no reason to suspect anything beyond that."

The crowd parted, more because Mr. Quinn and Samuel were bringing out the body than for anything my father had said. I heard someone mutter,

"But what was he doing wandering around in the middle of the night?"

Getting a glass of water? Heading for the privy? Running away from a shadow on the window? *There was no way we'd ever know,* I thought. Not for sure.

The crowd was breaking up, Annabelle was off looking for either Charity Pickett or Elijah Quinn, and I had no place special to go, when I heard a voice call out, "Ben!"

Zandra came running up to me, her skirts looking even more colorful in the bright sunshine than they had two days earlier. She motioned for me to join her, out of the way of other people, in the alleyway between the hotel and Pickett's General Store.

"I thought you'd be long gone," I said with a glance to the people who were giving us—her—dirty looks. "But, still, it's good to see you again."

"We're leaving now," Zandra said. "It's not safe for us here anymore." She gestured vaguely toward the street, indicating she meant not safe because of the townspeople, rather than not safe because of a crazed, bloodthirsty ghost. "My mother sent me to find you, and I'd nearly given up."

I was torn between being hurt that she hadn't answered, "It's good to see *you*, too," and wanting to say that it wasn't fair people were making

Zandra's family feel they had to move on, and being curious about why Zandra's mother would send her to find me. Curiosity won. "Your mother? Why—"

"Listen to me," she interrupted. "I told her about what happened last summer—with that man, Jake Barnette—and about the readings I did for you and Annabelle."

This was not going to be good news, I could tell. "And?" I asked.

"And she did a reading for Jake Barnette."

That was not something I would ever have guessed. "Jake is dead," I said. "How can he have a future to read?"

Zandra ignored that. She said, "She kept getting cards that told of cruelty, and bad choices, and use of power for destructive ends."

I shivered, despite the sunshine. "That sounds like Jake," I said. What else *could* I say?

Zandra punched my arm. "You're not listening. The outcome card was the World. *Reversed.*"

Obviously she figured even I should see the significance of that. "Reversed" meant upside down, I remembered that. The world upside down? I didn't understand. "What does that mean?" I asked.

"An earthbound spirit attached to one place."

In the silence that hung between us, I heard a

man around the corner on the street calling, "Zandra! Zandra!"

Zandra glanced over her shoulder, but she didn't answer. "We heard about the two recent deaths," she told me in a whisper, as though she didn't dare speak out loud.

Of course, they'd heard. People were saying it was the tinkers' fault: the tinkers had brought the rain, the rain had swelled the river, the water had released Jake's coffin and therefore Jake.

Zandra said, "My mother said to tell you, 'Be careful.' A man like that, a promise like that. . . . There's great power involved here, Ben."

Out on the street, a second voice added to the first calling for Zandra, a child, I guessed.

Zandra yelled something over her shoulder in her foreign language, probably, "Just a minute," because she took hold of my shoulder and spoke all in a rush. "My mother says the closer he comes to fulfilling his promise, the more powerful he'll get—the more life he'll get."

"What's that mean?" It seemed I was always asking her that.

She punched me again. "*Listen,*" she insisted.

I *was* listening. I just wasn't understanding.

She said, "My mother says he can come back. If you let him do this, he can come back."

"'Let him'?" I repeated. "'Do this'? You mean if

I *let him* kill me?" I asked. "I wasn't planning on letting him—" I stopped because she looked as though she were about to punch me again.

"If he comes back, there will be no stopping him," she said.

Just then a woman who had to be her mother came around the corner. Zandra's mother had hair that went out in all directions at once, which made her look kind of witchy. But she stopped when she saw me, and she must have known who I was, because—though she never said a word—she bowed her head, solemn and respectful, like I was dead already.

Zandra stepped away from me. "Good luck, Ben," she said.

That was it? Don't let Jake kill me? What kind of advice was that?

"But how can he be stopped?" I called after her.

"Bury him," Zandra said. "If it's not too late already."

Her mother put her arm around Zandra's waist to lead her away. Obviously someone wanted to get out of town in a hurry. Zandra looked back and gave a halfhearted wave. "Remember the Star," she said.

Star? I briefly considered the constellations, and then remembered the one good card Zandra had dealt in telling my fortune.

Now Zandra shook her head at me in disgust. She said something to her mother, then came running back to me. She dug into her pocket, pulled out her fortune-telling cards, and hastily looked through them. "Here." She shoved the Star card at me. Then, without another word, she turned and ran to catch up to her mother.

The Star, she had said, *that means hope, and love which will help you.*

Stars. Hope. Love. I hoped she didn't mean Elijah and Samuel Quinn's cousin, Naomi. In school she *had* taken recently to smacking the back of my head with her ruler, which I supposed *could* be an early sign of love. Though I was willing to take any help I could get, I hated the thought of having to count on Naomi.

I looked at the card in my hand. There were stars, and a woman emptying two jugs of water. Was it supposed to help me or reassure me? It wasn't much in either case.

"Will you ever come back?" I called after Zandra. "When people calm down and get sensible again? They will, you know," I promised her.

She looked over her shoulder to say, "We travel. Some places we come back to."

"I'll be here," I told her, meaning we *didn't* travel. But then I thought about it: *I'll be here*.

Unless, of course, I wasn't.

Graveside Ceremonies

I sat on the sample casket Quinn and Sons Mortuary keeps in front to serve as a bench and waited for Pa. I tried to figure a way—without mentioning ghosts or fortune-telling cards—to convince him that we needed to get Jake back in the ground as quick as possible. But when Pa finished in there and saw me, it turned out he had the same idea.

"Run fetch Pastor Pratt," he told me. "I know Barnette was buried proper already the first time, but the way things are going, it can't hurt for people to see him laid into the ground with a strong new blessing."

"Right, Pa," I said.

"Bury all this foolishness with him," he muttered.

"Right, Pa," I repeated. But I didn't think it was foolishness. Any hope that it was foolishness had disappeared that morning with Judge Wade dead at the foot of the stairs.

The news of what Pa planned spread fast. Within the hour that it took for Pastor Pratt to finish his breakfast, get dressed, gather what he needed, and show up at the cemetery, half the town was there already, set to give Jake Barnette a proper send-off.

I thought it was a good thing Zandra and her family were already gone. From some of the ugly talk I'd overheard, it sounded to me as though the townfolk were ready to give the tinkers a proper send-off, too. People always want to have *someone* to blame their troubles on.

In the cemetery, patches of the ground were still squishy wet. The other coffins wouldn't be reburied until the following day.

Mr. Quinn, being the undertaker and an expert in such matters, chose the new burial site. He recommended that none of the coffins that had come up should go back where they'd started, just in case the river ever flooded again, even though it had never flooded before. But in Jake Barnette's case, Mr. Quinn chose the highest, driest corner, as far away from the river as possible.

Pastor Pratt said a blessing over the land, which hadn't actually been part of the cemetery before, then he blessed the men who were going to do the digging; he even blessed the shovels.

The gravediggers took the time to dig the hole for Jake eight feet deep, rather than the customary six. And once they were finished, Pastor Pratt blessed the hole, too.

The only thing left to bless was Jake Barnette himself, in his coffin.

We all moved to the spot where Pa and Emmett Sanders had set down Jake's coffin two days earlier.

Pastor Pratt said another prayer.

We all said "Amen" with extra feeling.

Pa and Emmett bent their knees and grabbed hold of the coffin's handles. As the coffin lifted off the ground, muddy water came running out from where the boards were joined.

Elijah Quinn and Annabelle wiggled their eyebrows at each other. Most of the people had disgusted grimaces on their faces. I know *I* did, at the thought of the probable condition of Jake Barnette's corpse.

Pa and Emmett took a few steps, but they were both frowning, like they were puzzling on something, and their steps got hesitant, and then they stopped.

"Is something wrong?" Mr. Quinn asked.

"It seems too light," Pa said.

"He's been in there almost nine months," Elijah

said. Then, for the benefit of those too squeamish to follow his reasoning, he added, "I expect he's pretty much rotted away by now."

His father smacked him on the side of the head, while several of the women fanned themselves with their handkerchiefs.

Pa shook his head. "But it was heavy two days ago."

Pastor Pratt said, "Surely that was because of all that water. . . ."

But Pa and Emmett were looking at each other with a look that made my stomach go all funny.

Bury him, Zandra's voice whispered in my memory. *Bury him. Bury him. If it's not too late already.*

They set the coffin back down on the ground, and Mr. Quinn crouched beside it. He ran his hand over the edge where it was nailed shut. He shook his head. "This hasn't been tampered with," he assured everyone.

I think we all believed him.

But I don't think any of us were reassured.

Mr. Quinn stood and gripped one of the handles. Emmett lifted the other end.

Mr. Quinn got that same funny look on his face.

"Anybody happen to have brought a crowbar?" Pa asked.

They ended up bringing the coffin back to the hole that had just been prepared for it. There, they used the shovels to pry the lid open. The wood screeched along the nails, setting my teeth on edge—as if the coffin opening wouldn't have done that on its own.

Except for a smear of mud glistening on the bottom, the coffin was empty.

13

Three of Swords

They covered the coffin back up, partly because everyone figured a used coffin shouldn't be left open, and partly—I think—because we were all sort of hoping Jake was really still in there and that we just couldn't see him.

Then everybody went home, fast, leaving me, Annabelle, Pa, and Emmett Sanders. I suspect people feared that Jake Barnette might send bolts of lightning to get the four of us, and nobody wanted to be standing too close, just in case.

Back at his office, Pa told us, "There's a perfectly reasonable explanation for all this." Then he sighed. Loudly. "But I have no idea what it could be." He rested his head in his hands.

"Zandra said there was magic coming," Annabelle said. She no longer seemed to find all this amusing. "Magic and sorrow and changes. Lots of changes."

"Who's Zandra?" Emmett asked.

Pa raised his head. He ignored Emmett and asked us, "What else did she say?"

"That Jake Barnette is getting stronger and stronger," I told him. "And that we should have buried him while there was still time."

"Where is this girl, Zandra?" Pa asked.

"Gone." Why did I feel as though she'd abandoned us? She had no call to stay. And even if she *had* stayed, what power did she have besides the ability to see our doom coming? I said, "She and her family left town this morning. They were worried about people blaming them."

"Why don't we go, too?" Annabelle suggested.

"The four of us?" Pa asked, including Emmett with a wave of his hand, since we were all in this together. I was nodding, too. He continued, "Pack up everything, start all over again someplace where we don't know anybody, and assume—" He bit off what he had started.

"What?" I asked.

Pa looked away. He hated to admit it, but he finished, "That someone who can travel back from the grave can't cross town lines?"

I hadn't thought of that.

Annabelle started to cry, and Pa pulled her to him in a hug. "We'll stay together," he said. "The four of us. He can't get all four of us at once,

Annie, can he? He went after each of the others when they were alone. We'll protect each other. All right?" He wouldn't let her go until she nodded. Until I nodded. "All right," he repeated firmly.

So we stayed together all day: first in the sheriff's office all morning, then for lunch to Mrs. Pratt's boardinghouse, where Emmett had a room, then back to Pa's office for the long, long afternoon. Nobody dropped in at the office to visit, and nobody sat near us during lunch; and when we walked home in the evening, Elijah Quinn crossed the street to avoid us, loyal friend that he was.

Emmett came home with us.

"We'll stand watch all night," Pa said, "Emmett downstairs and me up. Annabelle will sleep in your room, Ben." He ruffled my hair, which in normal circumstances I would have complained against. "Nothing and nobody is getting in here," Pa assured us.

"You going to stand there just looking at us while we sleep?" Annabelle asked.

I didn't think I could sleep in those circumstances either. But Pa said he'd be in the hall, with our door open.

I wasn't especially scared at that particular moment, and Annabelle didn't seem to be either, since it was only just turning dark outside. I guess we figured whatever was coming would come in the still of the night. So Emmett was in the kitchen washing up the supper dishes, and Pa was going from room to room lighting a lamp in each so there wouldn't be any dark corners anywhere, when Annabelle suddenly remembered she'd left the photograph of Mama in her room. And that *did* scare her a bit, I could tell, the idea of going along that length of hallway all by herself to fetch it.

"I'll get it," I offered. I didn't say "*Since you're scared to.*" I said, "That will give you time to change into your nightdress."

Pa had already lit the light on her nightstand, and I found the picture right beside it. There we all were in our Sunday best. I looked so young it was hard to believe it really *was* me, except I remembered the photographer sticking his head under his black cloth, the flash of light, the lingering smell of powder. There was Annabelle, with her blurry foot. And Pa, with more hair than he'd had in a few years. And, of course, Mama.

We were all serious in the picture, but whenever I thought of Mama I always remembered her laughing. The picture being black and white, her dress looked white, but it had really been palest blue. It smelled of cedar, because she only wore it for special, and she'd taken it out of the chest shortly before the photographer arrived. It was the dress that, two years later, she'd been buried in.

I headed back with the picture. In my room, Annabelle was sitting on my clothes chest under the window, not changed yet after all, which was supposed to be why she'd stayed behind. Instead, she was busy rummaging through a box of my things, snooping. What she had in her hand was the Star card Zandra had given me. I knew what Annabelle would say: *Oooo, love.* And I knew who she'd say it to: Elijah Quinn. To start with. I'd never hear the end of it.

I opened my mouth, but before I got a chance to call her a sneaky little wretch, I saw something that froze the words into a solid lump in my throat. Right behind her, his face pressed against the window, was Jake Barnette.

The picture dropped from my fingers and hit the floor with a crash that shattered the glass of the frame.

Jake's gaze moved from the back of my sister's head to meet my eyes.

He wasn't all rotted away, the way Elijah Quinn had said, and he wasn't all faint and wispy the way I'd always pictured ghosts. Except for the fact that he was muddy from the water that had seeped into his coffin, he looked pretty much like he must have when they laid him in there. But his neck was obviously broken, his head flopped to one side just the way Elijah had mimed it for us the day of the hanging. The rope still dangled from his neck, though I doubted they had really buried him that way.

Annabelle had jerked up at the sound of the picture frame breaking, and she saw where I was looking. She whirled around, but one glance at Jake and she couldn't move either.

Pa's voice called from his room down the hall, "Everything all right in there, Ben?"

Jake grinned at us, with his head all lopsided. He touched the glass just inches from Annabelle's face, leaving a muddy smear.

"Ben?" Pa called again, sudden anxiety in his voice.

The muscles in my throat were too tight to get a sound out. It was like in a bad dream, when you know if you could just holler out, you'd wake yourself up, but still you just can't. Except that I knew this was no dream.

"Annabelle?" I heard Pa step out into the hall.

Jake apparently didn't need to hold on to anything to float up there grinning into the second-story window. He put his finger to his lips, like we were all in on a secret.

Pa was coming down the hall toward us; I could hear his footsteps falling heavy as he approached at a near run.

And then he was shoving me out of his way.

"Annie—*down!*" he commanded. I don't know if he'd drawn his gun before entering the room or after seeing Jake, but it was in his hand now.

Annabelle flung herself off the chest and onto the floor.

The gun roared. The window shattered, taking the smear of mud with it. But not Jake Barnette. He still hung there, grinning. With the hand he'd used to touch the window, he pointed at each of us—Annabelle, me, Pa—and his lips formed the silent words: *And you. And you. And you.*

And then, finally—solid as he'd seemed—he dissolved into the surrounding blackness.

Pa hugged us close to him. None of us said a word or made a sound. I could still smell the gunpowder, the way I'd been able to smell the flash powder from the photographer. Outside, a couple of dogs who'd heard the gunshot were barking. Neighbors' doors were banging open.

And in the silence of the house, his voice shaking because the house *was* so silent, finally Pa called, "Emmett?"

14

"Emmett?" Pa called again, more forcefully this time.

Still no answer.

Emmett had to have heard the commotion. There was the possibility that he was too scared to come upstairs. But I didn't think that was likely.

Pa got loose from Annabelle, who was clinging to him. "If something's happened to Emmett," he said, "we're certainly not safe huddled together up here."

The way I looked at it, if hanging and drowning and being hit pointblank by a bullet didn't slow Jake down, we weren't safe anywhere.

"I'll go first," Pa said, even though Annabelle was shaking her head frantically. "Ben will come last so he can warn us of anything coming up behind. You'll be safe in the middle, Annie." She was still shaking her head, but he went right on talking. "Stay real close, but don't hang on to me in case I need to move fast."

Then he went to the door, which was more effective than any argument he could have used. Annabelle certainly wasn't going to let him leave her behind.

I caught hold of the sleeve of her dress near her elbow so she could feel me there behind her. "I'm here," I told her, and we stepped out into the hall.

"Emmett?" Pa called from the top of the stairs.

All we could hear was a faint tapping. Not one of the neighbors come checking on us, I was sure. They probably already figured they *knew* what the commotion was. And they'd be right. Now they'd wait for us to come out, or till morning. If then. But that was sort of what it sounded like, someone with a lot of patience come calling. *Tap-tap.* Then maybe five or six seconds. *Tap-tap.* Or, sometimes, just one: *Tap.*

We headed down the stairs, which was definitely not where I wanted to go. But I was with Annabelle in this case: I definitely didn't want to stay upstairs, either.

The lamps Pa had lit were still burning. Not a dark corner in the house.

But it was still spooky.

"Emmett?" Pa called.

The tapping was louder down here. Outside, the neighbors had hushed their dogs.

Pa was holding his gun ready, even though it hadn't had much effect upstairs. Like in a game of follow the leader, we made our way across to the kitchen, the last place any of us had seen Emmett. At the closed door, Pa motioned for Annabelle to back off a step.

"You're doing fine," I told her. I took a deep breath, so I would be inhaling, so I wouldn't embarrass myself, yelling out at whatever awful thing we'd see in there.

Then Pa kicked the door open.

Nobody there.

The dishes were all washed. Some of them were still draining on the sink; others, dried, were set on the table, ready to be put away. The towel was in the pot, as though Emmett had been in the middle of drying it. The back door was open.

So, I figured Emmett *had* fled at the sounds of trouble upstairs. I figured the tap-tap was the door swinging in the wind.

But then it came again—*tap-tap*—and the sound wasn't from the kitchen. Maybe from the parlor, which was the room next to us, or from outside.

Pa headed for the open door.

I dragged on Annabelle's sleeve, because she had a tendency to want to hold on to his belt, and that could prove a fatal distraction to him. But I sure wasn't planning to let him get more than a couple of steps ahead.

From the doorway, Pa checked all around before stepping outside, and so did we. The night was dark, and apparently crickets aren't afraid of ghosts—that was about all I learned.

Carefully we made our way around the corner of the house, hugging close to the walls. This is the side of the yard that the parlor looks out on, and Annabelle's room, which is directly above.

There was the old elm tree Annabelle used for her secret escapes.

And there was the cause of the tapping we'd heard.

For there was Emmett Sanders—hanging by his neck from one of the lower branches, the toes of his boots bumping against the parlor window.

Pa jammed his gun back in its holster and ran to put his shoulder up under Emmett's butt, to support his weight while he tried to loosen the noose and get it up over Emmett's head.

Too late, too late, I thought. *I* could see Emmett was already dead. Why couldn't Pa?

Emmett had been close to being a friend, for all that he was a grown-up and I wasn't. But all I felt—or, at least the strongest thing I felt—was that we had to get out of there.

Then, just as Pa was off-balance reaching for the rope, Jake Barnette stepped forward, almost as though materializing from out of the tree.

"Pa!" Annabelle and I both yelled.

But before Pa could react, Jake drove his elbow into the side of Pa's head. Pa staggered, and Jake hit him again. Jake was a big guy, but I always figured Pa was wiry and strong. Still, the third time Jake hit him, Pa fell and didn't get up again. Then Jake lifted the noose from his own neck. It caught on his ear because his head was still too heavy for his broken neck, and then I saw him turn toward where Pa was lying on the ground.

Never mind that if Pa couldn't stop him, what good could I do? I went running up because I couldn't just stand there and let Jake Barnette kill my father. I wasn't even aware of falling; just suddenly I was sitting several feet back from where I last remembered being, my ears ringing. Jake was leaning over my father, tightening the noose around his neck.

Miss Hawkes always said I had more stubbornness than sense. I got to my feet and jumped onto Jake's back, aiming to tighten my arms around his neck. He backed into the tree, the way a bear will, and smacked me against the trunk again and again until I lost my wind and couldn't hold on any longer.

Then he leaned over Pa again.

Pa was just beginning to come to. He got his hands up to the rope, but Jake dragged back on it, cutting off Pa's air.

All this while, Annabelle was hollering. But I knew—and she probably knew it, too—that none of our neighbors were going to risk trying to help us: what could they do to stop a dead man, anyway?

Jake threw the loose end of the rope over the same branch that held Emmett and pulled, jerking Pa to his feet. And pulled again, so that Pa's feet left the ground.

I hit the back of Jake's knee. The leg buckled, but he didn't fall. He turned around, which momentarily set Pa's feet back on the ground. I could see Jake was going to kick, and I tried to roll out of the way but didn't move fast enough. His foot caught me in the ribs. Then—as I lay panting—he again tugged the rope that was around Pa's neck. He was going to kill Pa, then he was going to kill Annabelle, then he was going to kill me. I *knew* that was the way it was going to be, that was the order he was going to do it, because I couldn't think of anything worse than lying there, helpless, seeing it all happen.

Something moved in front of my face, gauzy white. I thought I was in the middle of passing out, because I couldn't hear Annabelle screaming anymore, and I figured sight and hearing were going, and I wasn't going to live long enough to miss them. *Good,* I thought. I wasn't going to fight to hold on, to watch Pa and Annabelle die. But then I heard a thump, which was Pa hitting the ground: Jake had let go of the rope.

Finally my eyes focused.

It wasn't white I'd seen; it was palest blue.

By the light of the parlor window I could see a woman struggling with Jake. Unlike Jake, she *was* faint and wispy. But though her hands passed through him, and his through her, she was having more effect on him than any of us had. Jake was holding the hand he'd tried to strike her with, cradling it now, as though the almost-contact had hurt. He flinched and held up his left arm to protect himself from her insubstantial blows, and he was backing away.

And there was a scent in the air that reminded me of the cedar chest.

"Mama?" I whispered. *Mama* was Zandra's 'love who would help' me? But then I realized: if Jake's hate could bring Jake back, why couldn't Mama's love bring Mama back?

Pa was making strangling sounds, and I finally found the sense to rush to his side, to help loosen the rope so he could breathe. Pa shoved at me—not hard, because he didn't have the strength to manage that, but away. "Annabelle," he whispered, his voice raw from the rope.

I glanced around. Not a sign of her. Pa shoved again. What did he want? I should stay and help.

Stay and help what? I asked myself. I'd already seen there was nothing I could do to slow down Jake Barnette, and what would it serve to drag Pa back into the house, even if I could manage his weight, when Jake could follow us in?

Except that Jake wasn't doing very well. Jake was huddled on the ground with his back against the wall of the house, becoming less and less solid each time Mama touched him, looking like whitewash when you keep adding water.

Where *was* Annabelle?

And suddenly I knew.

15

Graveside Ceremonies, Part 2

I ran as fast as I could. I caught up to Annabelle in the street outside of Pa's office, but I figured *she* could catch up to *me* farther on. I ran past the school, past the church. I ran past the cemetery to the high dry area that would be the new part of the cemetery. The area that—so far—had only one grave site, unused. So far.

Jake Barnette's coffin sat at the edge of the hole that had been dug for it. *Bury him,* Zandra's mother had told Zandra to tell me. We had thought it was too late. And Jake being what he was and the rest of us being what we were, we hadn't been able to stop him. But Mama being what *she* was, maybe she could hold on to him long enough. Annabelle had seen that first, clever girl. But I usually do catch on, eventually.

I dug my boots into the muddy earth and threw

my weight against the coffin. It moved, slightly, closer to the edge. I shoved more. The corner dipped into the ground and jammed.

I could hear Annabelle, her feet slapping on the ground, her breath wheezing, as she approached. I went around to the other side of the coffin, being careful not to fall into the hole myself, and pulled up on one of the handles to unwedge the corner. It sure seemed heavy enough to be holding a body to me.

"Ready," I gasped to Annabelle.

She shoved and I pulled and the coffin slid till part of it was overhanging the hole.

So far, so good, except that now there was no way I could hold on to it any longer without being ten feet tall and standing in the hole itself. So much for pulling. I moved back around next to Annabelle and we both heaved.

Again.

Again.

The coffin balanced on the edge of the hole, half of it extending over empty air. I reached out as far as I could and pushed on the top of it. Like a teeter-totter with a fat kid on one end, the coffin tipped down, down, raising the end we'd been pushing. And then the coffin toppled into the hole, settling almost flat, but upside down.

I ran to the pile of dirt that had been shoveled

out of the hole. The gravediggers had taken their shovels home with them, but I began pushing at the top of the pile.

When the first clumps of dirt hit the coffin lid, there was an awful scream from inside it. I shuddered as the box shook, as it was pounded from the inside.

I froze.

Annabelle scrambled up next to me and began flinging handfuls of dirt on the coffin, ignoring the screams.

I set my teeth and joined her.

As soon as there was a layer of dirt completely covering the coffin, even though in places it couldn't have been more than a pebble thick, the screams stopped.

We kept on shoveling with our hands as long as we could, which wasn't really very long. Annabelle sank to an exhausted heap, and I gave out shortly after, my hands hurting from digging, my head hurting where Jake had hit me, my ribs hurting where he'd kicked me.

I crouched in the dirt, looking down at the hole, thinking how strong Jake had been when he knocked me and Pa around, and how surely I shouldn't stop until there were at least a couple of feet of dirt on top of the coffin's lid holding it in place. I was only waiting to regather my strength, but then I heard Annabelle whisper, "Mama."

I looked up and saw Mama crouched there beside us, and I figured that meant we were safe. She reached out her hands, brushing her fingers, soft and real, against our cheeks, mine and Annabelle's. And then she was gone, leaving only a faint scent of cedar behind.

Pa recovered, though it took quite a while for the rope burns to disappear completely from his neck.

Annabelle and I were heroes at school for about a week, until Elijah Quinn broke his arm falling off the roof of the Pratts' barn, which he was walking across on a dare. After that, he was the center of attention until. . . . I can't remember: somebody else did something.

The old coffins all got reburied, along with the new ones for Mr. Chetwin, Judge Wade, and Emmett Sanders. So far, they've all remained buried.

The morning after Jake tried to kill us all, we found the Star card that Zandra had given me. We found it, when we went to bury Jake Barnette one final time, beside his grave, where Annabelle and I had seen Mama. How it got there, we don't know for sure. *I* certainly didn't bring it with me, and Annabelle says she didn't bring it with her. In fact, I remember seeing it in Annabelle's hand when I walked into my room and found her sitting on my clothes chest with only the glass of the window between her and Jake Barnette. I remember dropping the picture frame, and Annabelle's startled and guilty expression, and how she turned and saw Jake. I *think* I remember seeing the card flutter from her fingers to the floor.

But while everybody believes in Jake, nobody seems much inclined to believe in Mama. Pa, they say, was injured and doesn't know what he saw, and Annabelle and I are just children. They say Annabelle must have been carrying that card, and she dropped it when she and I stopped Jake by throwing dirt on his coffin.

That morning, burying Jake, I considered throwing the card into his grave, in case that would be likely to help hold him in there. But then I decided to trust. So I kept the card, to return to Zandra. I haven't yet seen her again, but I still hope she and her family do come back someday. I have to admit, though, maybe the town isn't quite ready yet.

And we never yet saw Mama again, either. But sometimes, when I'm in trouble, I could swear I smell cedar nearby.